When Fields Hum & Glow

by

Blythe Ayne

When Fields Hum & Glow

by

Blythe Ayne

Books & Audio by Blythe Ayne

Nonfiction:
Love Is The Answer
45 Ways To Excellent Life
Life Flows on the River of Love
Horn of Plenty–The Cornucopia of Your Life
Finding Your Path, Engaging Your Purpose

How to Save Your Life Series:
Save Your Life With The Power Of pH Balance
Save Your Life With The Phenomenal Lemon
Save Your Life with Stupendous Spices
Save Your Life with the Elixir of Water

Absolute Beginner Series:
Write Your Book! Publish Your Book! Market Your Book!

Fiction:
The Darling Undesirables Series:
The Heart of Leo - short story prequel
The Darling Undesirables
Moons Rising
The Inventor's Clone
Heart's Quest

Novellas & Short Story Collections:
5 Minute Stories
Lovely Frights for Lonely Nights
When Fields Hum And Glow

Children's Illustrated Books:
The Rat Who Didn't Like Rats
The Rat Who Didn't Like Christmas

Poetry:
Home & the Surrounding Territory

Audio:
The Power of pH Balance –
Dr. Blythe Ayne Interviews Steven Acuff

Dedication:

*To all who are willing
To suspend disbelief....*

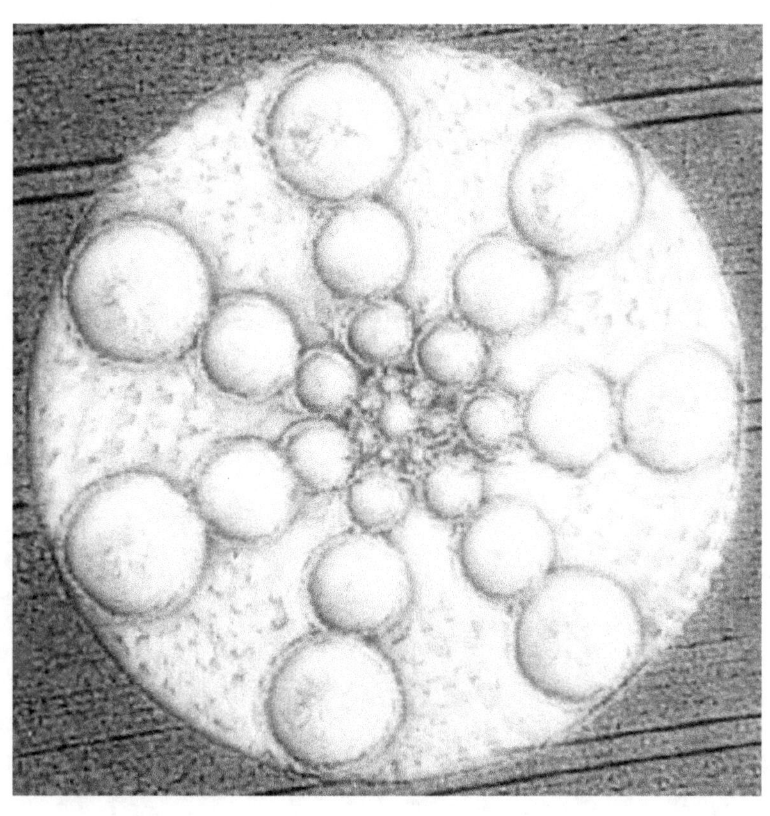

Emily stepped out the back door of the farmstead to watch dusk fall with a gentle yet great sigh across the rolling hills. It'd been a hot, sultry day in July in Englanhhd's Pewsey Vale. An unusual cast of orange and lavender clouds finally relented their hold on the horizon, while a chilled, puckish breeze played across Emily's bare forearms and face.

She needed a deep breath of coolness and a respite from her husband of six months and his grown children, all of them bickering over something his first wife, their mother, had said or not said ten years ago, as she lay slowly dying.

Meandering across the back yard, Emily told herself at every step to return. But her feet willed themselves forward, passing the chickens bluck-blucking to one another in their shed, passing the cow barn, the day's heat emanating from the building, and walking beyond all the carefully tended and maintained buildings and grounds, out to the hedgerow in the tenebrous, shadowy evening.

She walked along the hedgerow to the wheat field and sank to the soft earth, wrapping her long skirt and her arms around her knees. She felt comforted and yet lonely among the acres of murmuring, fecund, heavy-headed grain.

She was wise enough to know she had a good life, but even so, this secure, gentle, respectable life did not keep her ennui at bay. She had an itch in her soul that no one and nothing had ever been able to scratch.

She cocked her head to better hear a shirring, humming sound coming from the field—a sound like none she'd ever heard. Could it be an insect? The sound grew in volume and intensity. Then she saw, suspended over the tops of the wheat, a dull red ball. As she focused on it, it became a swarming horde of red glowing bugs, moving slowly over the wheat.

The sound augmented. Stunned, confused, Emily watched small yellow sparks jump up from the heads of the wheat in a spiral formation, feeding into the dull red light swarm. A crackling emanated from the heads of wheat, a pulsing, electric charge, the smell of ozone oozed into the air.

Orange globes the size of pumpkins materialized, zig-zagging crazily among the little yellow sparks. White tubes floated among the globes. A grating sound, like hundreds of traction toys grinding away at once, manifested—Emily saw that the sound came from black cones, only visible when crossing one of the weird lights. *The noises!* There was a trilling, like a huge line being pulled out, warbling and whistling across the field, before, behind, under and around her. A vacuum-wind whirled at her.

Other lights flashed in the field—orange, red, green—flickering rapidly. The heady floral fragrances of hyacinth, lavender, gardenia and freesia overtook the night. Dark Y-shaped rods jumped up and down in mid-air beating the wheat down, laying it flat.

Then, shockingly, suddenly, all fell still. Deathly silent. Dark. No breeze, no fragrance, and not a single nocturnal creature sound. No crickets, no frogs. No sound, whatsoever.

Emily felt a strange pressure as if in a hermetically sealed bell-jar.

Befogged, confused, the sound of her own breathing echoed noisily around her. Finally, a sense of the mundane called to her, the back of her mind demanded her attention and suggested she return to the house. She rose unsteadily to her feet, hoping Daniel's adult children had left—mystified by her commonplace thought in the midst of such great mystery.

Moving slowly, with a stilted grace, Emily found her way back to the hedgerow. In her periphery, she felt more than saw a presence … something beyond words or thoughts or feelings. As she turned, a huge yellow-white spinning disc came out of the sky, a ferris wheel on its side, spinning madly until all its lights were a blur, accompanied by a sound at a timbre beyond hearing.

Emily felt the sound in her skeleton, in her blood, in the gelatinous humor of her eyeballs. She crumpled to her knees as the swirling power created an electrical vortex—she heard her skin crackle as the wheat had done. So beyond fear as to nearly feel nothing, Emily took in what she saw. A disc, made of two huge, curved plates, back to back, the top one whirled clockwise, the bottom one anti-clockwise.

It's as big as the barn, Emily thought, trying in a trance-like way to attach concrete meaning to the vision.

The gigantic, rotating disc, moved intentionally and in an apparent pattern about the field. Then, suddenly, impossibly fast, it went straight up into the sky—smaller, smaller, smaller, until it winked out, lost in a deluge of stars.

* *

*T*yi wrote on his granite tablet with his finger, recording that the foundational underpinning of the agriglyph had been successfully manifested. Everything going smoothly. According to plan. Even the coincident witness was only a young woman, alone. If she tried to convince others of what she'd experienced, no one would believe her.

As usual.

* *

4 - When Fields Hum & Glow

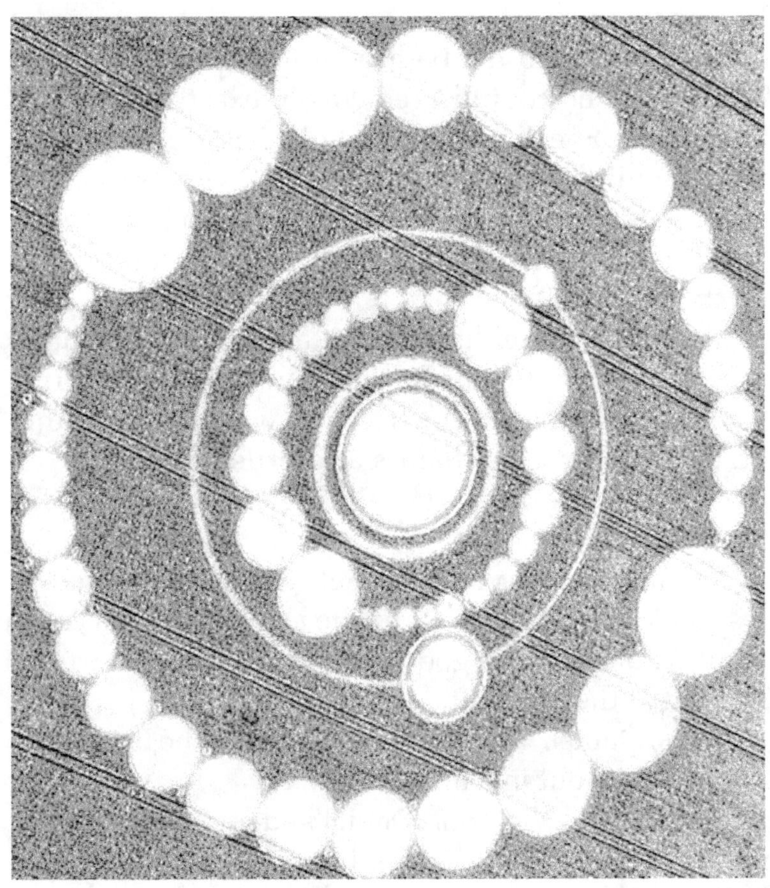

Emily stepped through the back door. She could hear the voices of her "step children" three people all her senior, coming from the living room. She glanced at the clock. 9:24. She'd left the house at 8:30. Less than an hour!

She went into the bathroom to study the mirror. Peculiarly, she couldn't remember, exactly, what she looked like. She flipped on the light. Yes, those features were familiar, but she did not *feel* the same—as if she saw her features through a foggy medium, as though her soul were on the outside and her physical features on the inside.

She washed her hands and face, then ran a comb through her luxurious dark brown hair, crepitating with so much static electricity it would only stand on end. She wet her hands and brushed them over her hair, smoothing it, calming herself with the gesture.

"Emily? Is that you?" Daniel called. She wanted to respond, "I'm not sure," but she *was* sure such a comment would not be a good idea, no matter how true it seemed at the moment.

"Yes, Daniel," she answered through the bathroom door. "I'll be out in a minute."

She heard Victoria, Daniel's daughter, say she needed to leave and that her husband, no doubt, had had enough of looking after the kids. Her younger brothers, Tim and Tom, thirty-eight year old twins, agreed, following Victoria's lead, like they always did. Victoria left directly, much to Emily's relief, but the twins lingered. She could no longer put off going out and saying good night to them.

She took one last study of the reflection in the mirror—same dark, full, shoulder-bobbed hair, same pouty mouth, same round, brown eyes—the blurring of soul and physicality slowly returning to what she knew as normal.

She stepped quietly into the living room, sat in the rocker by the dead fireplace, not listening to the rise and fall of conversation, but letting the knowable sanity of it wash over her. A remarkable exhaustion flooded her, as if she were drugged. She closed her eyes.

"Where did you go, Sweetheart?" Daniel ask. The boys remained very silent, always curious about how and or why this beautiful young woman, fifteen years *their* junior, had married their father. Though they told one another he deserved his happiness, they were also jealous, married to frumpy, uneventful wives.

"For a walk in the field."

"Hmmm," Daniel said, which everyone in the room knew meant how-very-strange-and-unlike-you-why-did-you-do-that?

The silence wore on.

Emily refused to attempt to tell these three skeptical men what had happened to her. They wore their pragmatism like hard-earned scout badges. She recalled the dinner when Victoria told the story of her mother having appeared to her a week after she died—the boys and their father almost hooted her out of the room. Emily saw Victoria blink back tears, while at the same time clamping her teeth tight.

"What did Mom tell you?" Tom—or was it Tim—had asked, sarcasm lacing his voice.

"That I was three weeks pregnant with her first grandchild, a spunky little girl with ginger hair like grandpa and a temperament like hers."

That shut the boys up, and Emily had watched a very pensive, curious expression grow on Daniel's features. Because Victoria *had* been newly pregnant when his first wife died. And the character of Rachel, Victoria's ginger-haired daughter, reminded them all, unnervingly, of Mother.

No one ever again mentioned the event.

"It's been such a hot day," Emily said, returning to the present. "I'm exhausted."

The boys appropriately took this to mean they ought to leave, and they did.

When she and Daniel were in bed, she couldn't keep from falling into a deep abyss of unconsciousness, and yet she felt herself trying to reach out to him, to touch her ordinary life, to hang onto the small, safe, real world, to escape the terrible and exciting knowledge of a reality beyond reality.

*   *

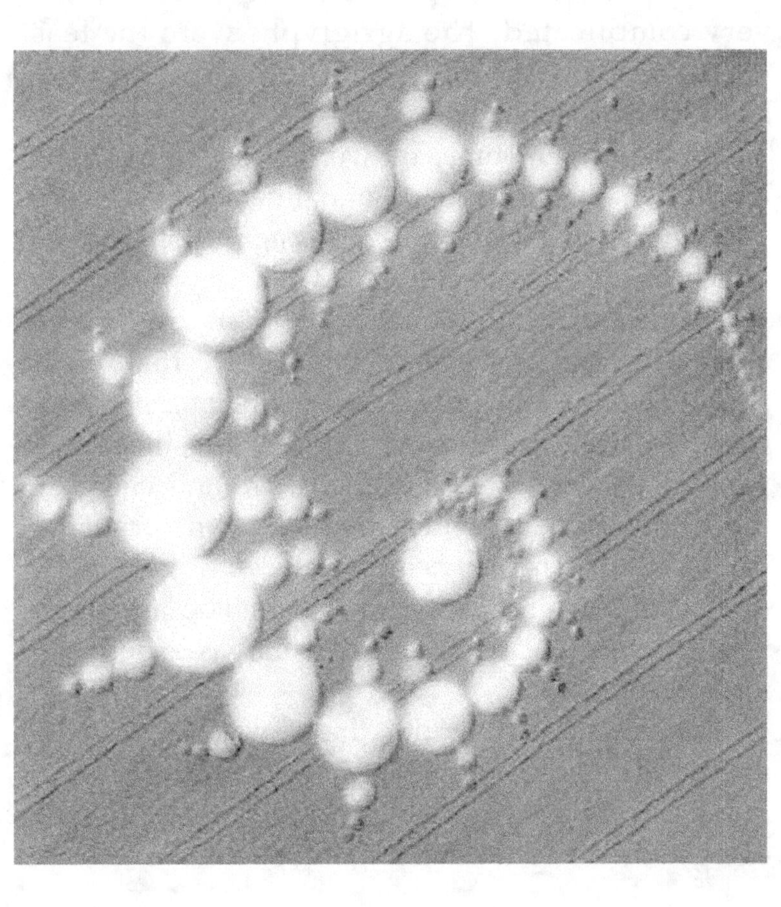

Tyi, the scribe, had four more agriglyphs to manifest that night. The Pharaohs and priests, the gods and goddesses, were returning in ever larger numbers, and the work became very complicated. The agriglyphs were the least of his responsibilities and duties in bringing back the hibernating gods.

At the present time, he worked on the return of Nodjme, a powerful, benevolent-but-demanding, Queen. She required him to manifest all her agriglyphs himself, which would take several nights to accomplish.

Tyi had come upon the idea of making people accomplish some of his work, at least certain of the agriglyphs of lesser priests. After directing people to create a particular set of crop circles, they themselves wondering where they got the desire and energy to tromp around all night, trespassing on farmlands, stomping out some very complicated, time-consuming designs, *Tyi* would charge the manmade agriglyphs which were acceptable with the plasma gasses necessary for transmutation.

But more often than not, the very specific location and design parameters planted in the little minds of humans went awry, and many of their attempts at the energy forms had to be disregarded.

* *

The next morning there was a pounding on the door, and, through the corridors of a deep, other-world, uncomfortable sleep, Emily thought she heard the voice of Bob, their neighbor.

"What in the name of the bad place ...." Daniel complained, gathering the energies of his tired, lean body.

Emily opened her eyes, cried out from the pain of the light streaming into the bedroom—the light which she usually loved more than any other part of the day.

Daniel looked over at her. "My God, Emily, your face! What ....? "

Bob hammered harder at the door. *"Daniel! Wake up!"*

"Am I dreaming?" Daniel said, turning and hurrying down the stairs, trying to pull his robe on as he went.

Squinting, Emily crept from the bed and over to the mirror. Her face was as red-pink as a peony, and swollen. She touched it gently. It looked and felt like a severe sun-burn.

She scurried to the window above the back door where Bob had been pounding, eaves-dropping on the conversation, though it wasn't the least bit hard to hear. Farmer Bob was worked up.

"The most amazing crop circle, Daniel. You're going to have thundering hordes tromping your wheat."

"Not if no one tells them," Daniel answered, ever logical.

"Tells them? You can see it from the road. There's all these circles with half circles and rings and lines connecting them, and, like, sort of arrows, and, well, you just need to look at it yourself. You should get someone out on the road to charge folks a pound. 'Cause that's the only way you're going to see your money out of those acres this season."

Emily could hear the skepticism in Daniel's voice as he tried to get Bob to calm himself, but the more Daniel spoke rationally and dispassionately, the more Bob's voice rose to counter Daniel's disbelief.

Emily pulled on jeans and a sweat shirt, then tip-toed downstairs and out the front door to view the phenomena that had their neighbor ranting at the crack of dawn.

Farmer Bob had not exaggerated. Across the side of the gentle slope of the hill Emily saw etched the design Bob had tried to describe. There was something about it particularly captivating, not just that it was so huge and unbelievably neatly done, but the symbol seemed to Emily to be something she knew, but could not remember.

Right then a passing car came to a screeching halt and a family poured out. Everyone exclaimed about the crop circle in a rowdy American accent of awe. The entire family started snapping shots on their phones and cameras as fast as they could. The husband nodded to Emily. "Boy, I'd sure hate to be the farmer who owns this place."

Emily managed a weak smile. "It'd be a challenge to have something like this on one's property."

"Are you kidding? Lookie-loos, new-agers, me-dia—that field's gonna get wasted—what a circus! A person should charge admission, that's what they should do. I tell ya, if we weren't on such a tight schedule, I'd go take a closer look myself."

"I guess I'd have to ask you a pound a head."

"Oh!" The man guffawed, and his wife gave an embarrassed grin. "It's yours, is it?"

"Well, the land it's on is. I have no idea who the symbol belongs to."

"*Ha!* Well, good luck with it, pretty lady. How long has it been there?"

"Ahm, about ten hours."

The man looked at her more closely. "Ten hours, eh? Did you ... make it?"

Emily tried to chuckle, but it came out a strange little non-verbal sound, like the sound a question mark would make if it could vocalize. "No. No, I certainly did not make it. But it wasn't there at sunset. And here it is, at sunrise."

The man nodded in agreement while his uncountable and unruly children ran about. Emily feared one or more of them were very likely to become flattened in the narrow road.

The man caught her glance. "Come on all you monsters, get back in the car."

"I beg ...." his wife began.

"Not you, my beautiful bride, creator of said monsters. Please, if you will, ensconce yourself in the carriage. We've got to get to London. Places to go, things to see." He herded his family back into the car, snapping a few more frames on his camera and phone as he went. "Thanks!" he called to Emily. Waving, he pulled away.

She nodded and waved back. "You're welcome," she replied softly. "But I didn't do anything." She turned, walked back up the road to the house and went in through the back door into the kitchen, just as Bob got in his truck and left, so distracted by looking at the field, he didn't even see her.

"Did you hear that?" Daniel asked. "The damnedest thing!"

"Yes, I heard Bob ranting. So I slipped out to look at it. He's not exaggerating. It's massive and entirely visible from the road."

"Maybe I *should* get a couple of the grandkids over to collect a few pounds."

"I believe that's a good idea—at least make an effort to discourage people from thinking they can roam around in your field as they please." Even as she spoke, calmly, rationally, Emily became aware of a feeling welling up inside her, a feeling of possessiveness, ballooning up, as if she would would wrap herself around the symbol and protect it from those who had no idea of its sacred importance.

Though she had no idea what its sacred importance was. She *did* know she didn't want anyone walking on it, taking pictures of it, wondering about it, casually, and surely, incorrectly, conjecturing what it meant, how it came to be. Or, even worse, as was often the case, blaming her poor, over-worked farmer husband of stomping down his own wheat in the night. As if he had nothing better to do, when all he ever needed was a good night's sleep.

In any case, she knew how the icon came to be there, in her husband's field. And she believed she knew who it belonged to.

It belonged to her.

Daniel studied Emily for a moment. "It must have been the way the sun was coming in the room or something, I could have sworn when I looked at you this morning, your face was red as a beet. But it's not now."

"Oh?" Emily looked at her reflection in the stainless steel toaster. Her face was hers again, not burned, not strange. Just, Emily. She shrugged. "You should go look at the field, Daniel, really."

"Sure, okay. Walk with me?" He held his hand out to her and together they strolled down the road. Already cars were stopping, people gawking, hanging out of car windows and standing on the road, taking hundreds of shots with with every device at hand.

"Holy priest!" Daniel exclaimed when he followed their gaze to the hillside. His sky-blue eyes filled with puzzlement, and his forehead furrowed like a newly plowed field. Emily had never seen her staid and unflappable husband this vexed. He turned his look of bemusement upon her. "You were out here last night. Did you ... did you *see* anything?"

Emily turned away from him to the revelation

imprinted on the golden grain. "I ... I think maybe I heard something strange," she half-lied lamely. She considered trying to tell him every, single detail of her experience the night before, and even share with him the strange, haunting dreams that had consumed her disturbed sleep. It would be a relief not to be alone with such a vast, and yet, inexplicable, experience.

But, something held her in check. She ... couldn't voice a syllable.

"Well, I'd just like to get my hands on the vandals who committed this crime, that's all I can say," he muttered in quiet undertones.

Emily knew Daniel well enough to know he'd decided how the icon had appeared, and he would not be changing his mind. She was wise to keep her experience to herself.

"Anyway, my dear, the way this ... art ... is stopping traffic, I think it's a good idea to get a couple of the kids over here to help you protect your interest. I have to head into town and get some groceries." Emily headed back to the house, and Daniel followed.

But once in Westbury, Emily made a beeline for the library, where she asked the librarian for information on crop circles. There was considerably more than she expected. She settled down and began poring over the materials. She read of sightings by people whose reports were nearly identical to what she'd say if she were to tell anyone what she'd seen, smelled, felt, heard, sensed, the night before. She read hypotheses by scientists, clergy, and crack pots. She read theories, speculations, historical parallels, and wild flights of fancy.

"Here, read this." A librarian handed Emily an unassuming-looking four page publication entitled *Plasmoids*. "I think you'll find it of particular interest."

Emily thanked her, a little surprised at the individual attention. She turned to the paper and read, "...*plasmas* are gasses which are largely ionized. Electrically neutral atoms are separated into negatively-charged electrons and positively-charged ions. The loss of the uniform electrical neutrality alters the behavior of the gas so that electric fields exist around the separated electrons and ions, and each field exerts force on the other charged particles. Accelerating charges create magnetic fields, which then exert their own force on the moving charges.

"The hydrodynamics, the motion of neutral particles, becomes complicated by electrodynamics and magnetodynamics. This convoluted bit of physics has come to be called *electromagnetohydrodynamics*, or EMHD.

"The *ponderomotive* force can be added to the mix, which is exerted on moving, charged, particles by electromagnetic radiation, which, in turn, is emitted by charged particles as they are accelerated by changing electric or magnetic fields. This creates a *plasma*.

"*Plasmas* may be luminous—the occasional recombinations of electrons with ions and the collisions of ions with ions release electromagnetic photons of visible light, also, potentially, thermal infrared radiation, radio waves, gamma rays and X-rays. A *plasma* may be audible in the crackle of coupling groups of electrons and ions, or in the low-frequency hum of pressure waves given off by an oscillating mass of ionized air. Examples of *plasmas* include: the nocturnal glow and buzz around high-voltage wires, the gas in a fluorescent light, the gas at the edge of a candle flame, the aurora borealis.

"*Plasmas* are everywhere."

Emily went up to the desk and asked if she could have a photocopy of the paper.

The librarian looked at it quizzically. "This isn't a library document," she said.

"But ... that other librarian gave it to me."

"Which librarian?"

"The one who ...." Emily paused. "That's strange, I can't for the life of me recall what she looked like. How very unlike me!"

The librarian returned the document to Emily. "I don't think a librarian handed this to you. If you want more information on plasmas, though, you might try the encyclopedia."

"Thank you." Emily stuck the *Plasmoid* paper in her purse, then stepped outside into the bright afternoon. "Just because you inform me of plasmas," she addressed the ether, "doesn't change my knowing that the ones I experienced last night were operated by an intelligence."

*   *

As Emily crested the last hill on the way home, she came upon a sideshow environment of cars parked crazily everywhere, children, dogs, and even adults, angling to become hood ornaments on one another's vehicles, swarming about like a haze of insects on the narrow country road. She looked across at the icon, and gasped at how it had already been ravaged by people, and dogs, and kids, everyone running about snapping endless pictures of one another grinning in the midst of the downed wheat.

It felt like a personal violation. Emily tried to let it go. Neither these people, nor the energy that created the icon, cared about her, had nothing at all to do with her, she told herself.

A queue lining up in front of a little card table, where sat a couple of Daniel's grandchildren along with some of their little friends that she didn't know, but who had the look of Farmer Bob stamped upon them with a cookie cutter simplicity, extracted a pound each from a willing, disorderly line of people.

The last thing she wanted to deal with at this moment was a horde of strangers. She waved to the children wanly as she worked her way around cars and turned in the driveway. She thought she spied both her husband and farmer Bob standing in the middle of the icon, milling about with the interlopers. Well, perhaps Daniel would recoup some of his financial losses from the trampled wheat, she reasoned as she hurried into the house with the groceries and put them away perfunctorily.

Then she grabbed the *Plasmoid* paper, ran up the two flights of stairs to her little attic sewing room, and locked the door—something she'd never done. She sat in the window seat that looked out upon the symbol etched in the grain. Despite the trampling abuse, the icon remained clear.

She held the *Plasmoid* paper, thinking she'd read it again. But she didn't. Instead, she thought, and thought, and thought, while the oak tree outside the window cast lengthening shadows across her lap and up her ribcage, embracing her. As she thought and gazed at the icon stretched out on the field, she let its message sink in. It informed her of something ... something ....

"Worlds within worlds," Emily whispered, studying the form in growing amazement, as she watched the icon slowly became animate, as if stretching itself after a long sleep.

The nesting circles moved along the line uniting them, and moved toward other circles. Then the entire pattern rose off the field and swirled about into a three-dimensional form in the air—the circles became globes, the lines and other geometric shapes came together like a giant puzzle knitting its pieces perfectly together. Though Emily saw the shape, it was like nothing she'd ever seen.

But more curious than that, she discovered herself *within* the shape—a part of the form! An intrinsic part of the form. As she hovered there, floating in the plasmoid, non-terrestrial medium, she watched as across from her materialized the stunning form of, well, Emily thought, a *goddess*.

*　*

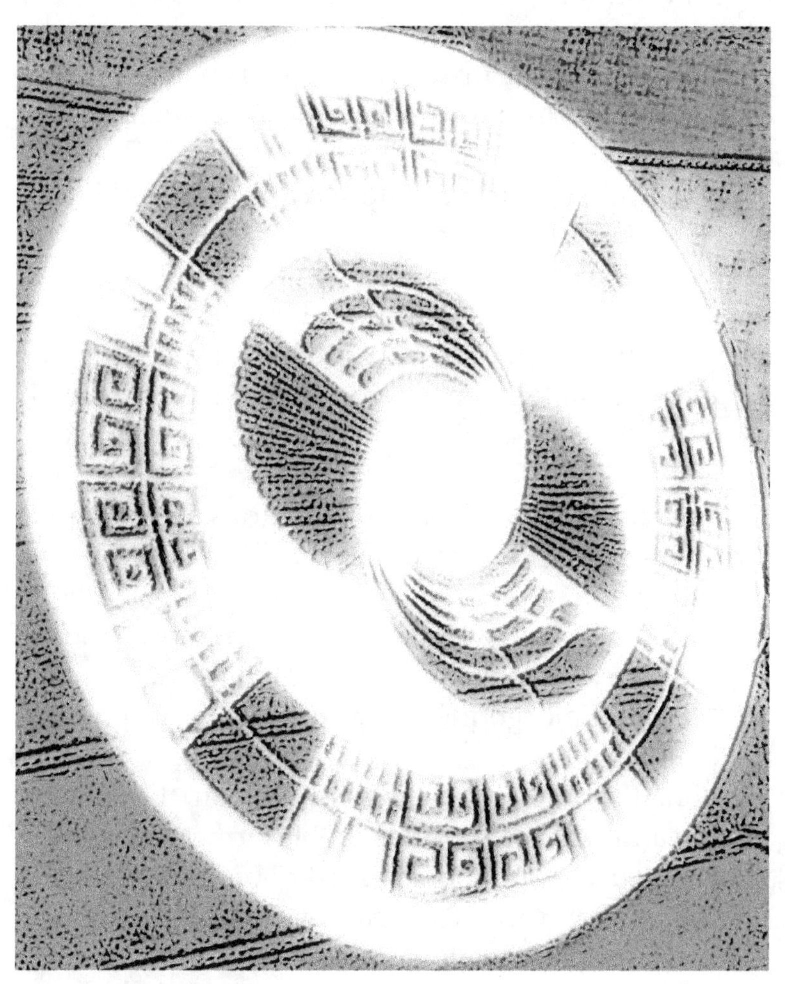

Nodjme crossed the dimensions through a gossamer plasma—tiny and exquisite, ethereal and translucent. Emily saw in the Goddess's eyes worlds and realities beyond comprehension.

She came right up to Emily, and insisted, "You cannot be here! You must relinquish your hold on the agriglyph."

"I ... I'm not holding onto anything. I don't know why I'm here." But, even as she spoke the words, Emily realized that she knew exactly why she was here. All her life she'd felt like she waited for something, that she had a purpose unfulfilled by her sweet-but-small, ordinary, country life. She paused, watching the mystical form of the goddess grow. A terrible beauty.

"*Release my agrigluph*," the goddess roared in a terrifying voice of many voices. "Don't you know who I am?"

"No," Emily answered simply. "Some sort of being from another dimension."

"I'm Nodjme, goddess and queen, the daughter of Amenhotep."

"Oh. I'm, ahh, pleased to meet you. I'm Emily, human and wife of Daniel, a humble farmer, who's field you've used for your icon. Yes, I do know of Amenhotep."

"Do not presume to speak of my father, the one true god, the greatest god of all gods."

"Ah, pardon me, angry goddess, but is he the one true god, or the greatest of gods? Because, properly speaking, they are opposite ...."

"Be quiet!" Nodjme fulminated.

Strange as it seemed to her, Emily could not keep quiet. She gave in to an uncontrollable compulsion to speak. "But, allow me to point out that even if you, yourself, are a god, then, well, then it seems your father could not be the only god."

Emily heard a soft chuckling, but she couldn't determine where it came from. Most assuredly it did not come from the angry goddess before her.

"How does one make you obey?" Nodjme shrieked. "Emily, wife of Daniel, *be quiet! And listen!* Your energy has become entangled in one of my transmutation agriglyphs. You must release your hold on the glyph. Your interference breaks the seal, the plasmas cannot be created, therefore, neither can I. And my time has come. You must let go."

Emily wanted to ask how was she holding on, and how could she let go. But she knew. She was holding on with desire, with her will.

"It's not that I don't fear you," Emily began. "I see that you're very powerful. And it's not that I don't revere you, because, even without knowing you, I sense your omnipotence. But I believe it's not an accident that I'm attached to the agriglyph. All my life I've felt that I was in the wrong place or the wrong body or the wrong time. Am I not, somehow, connected to you?"

"No. *You are not, little, insignificant human.* Although it's rare for a mortal to become entangled with the transmutation plasmas, and it's true that you're not an entirely usual human. But that does not make you one of us. We are not of the same materials. After I've transmuted, I'll be flesh and blood, but my life force is as different from yours, as yours is from a stone.

"I'm asking you to relinquish your hold as I have no desire to harm you. Other gods, I assure you, are never so kind. On occasion a human has become enmeshed in the transmutation energies. They rarely survive. Nor will you if you don't release that which is not yours."

The plasma around Nodjme roiled up, dark and threatening, while lightning streaked out in a halo around her, her arcane beauty, fascinating and frightening. Emily felt a peculiar chill as Nodjme's dark eyes fumed. And yet, she couldn't let go of that which she held on to by desire. Perhaps Nodjme deceived her. Emily could not give up her sense of fate, and how it had drawn her to the field last night, into the workings of supernatural powers.

It was her destiny!

"*No!*" a myriad thundering voices intoned. Emily felt as if her heart sank to her knees. "It is not your destiny, and you'll die this moment, your body will be found by your husband. He'll experience an unbearable grief, as he loves you more than himself. Silly woman! Live your own tiny but excellent life."

"I understand," Emily said, surprised at her own calm, facing death. But there were things she wanted—needed—to know. "I understand your threat. But what I don't understand is why you are returning to the three dimensions? Why are you and the others gods and goddesses becoming physical?"

Vexed, Nodjme flew in a circuit around Emily. Oh, curious!, Emily thought, I can see her all the way around, without turning my head.

"It's ... it's ... a vacation. In my usual form, I have many responsibilities, many duties. When I'm here, I put down all those obligations."

"*Oh!*" Emily said, truly surprised. "So ... you enjoy being here?"

"I would, if you would move out of my agriglyph so I can transmute."

"But I have another question." This was when Emily noticed a second figure in the brilliant halo that enclosed the agriglyph. Had he been there all along, or did he just materialize?

Nodjme turned to him in exasperation as if asking what was she to do.

Emily didn't see him speak, but she heard in her head, "Let us hear her question."

Nodjme turned to Emily. "Speak."

"Are gods always at war, like the myths insist, and like humans always are?"

"What a silly question! Of course not. There's no objective point to war. You may not under-stand this, but war does keep your species from developing. However, this is the way of lower life forms."

"I understand what you say, which is why I ask. But let me observe that the ancient Egyptian gods were always at war."

Nodjme returned to hovering before Emily, somewhat closer. "Oh, that's just a game. Like your video games. It's play, part of our vacation fun while on this world. We don't die of course. Just like a video game."

"I see!" Emily exclaimed. "So, as you are eternal, god-like beings, and when you die in a play war, you don't really die."

"Of course not."

"Because you're eternal beings."

"That's right." Nodjme looked again at the other figure, hovering in the light.

"Who is that?" Emily asked.

"That's Tyi, my high priest. He oversees my transmutation. But first, you *must leave*. You *must leave my agriglyph*."

A rapid crescendo of insight had begun flowing through Emily. "I understand now why I'm here, on Earth, and alive in this minute, in this plasmoid, in this agriglyph."

Nodjme grew to furious, gargantuan proportions, poised threateningly over her. "What is the matter with you? Do you not want to live?!"

Emily stayed focused. She wouldn't consider herself calm, but she *was* focused. "You say you are an eternal being. Well, I, too, am an eternal being."

"*Ha!*" Nodjme all but snorted. Most un-goddess-like, Emily thought. "You cannot compare us with you silly little mortals."

"Regardless, by your own admission—and, by the way, I already knew this without you telling me, but by your own admission—I'm an eternal being. So your threat to kill me if I don't comply with your demands is no real threat. The only difference will be that I'll be disembodied, and you'll have nothing left to threaten me with.

"Meanwhile, the eternal me will still be in your plasmoid, will still have a hold on your agriglyph. You'll not be able to come into the three dimensions and play with all your god friends, if I correctly understand what you've told me." Emily watched the exchange between Nodjme and Tyi. He gave her a look that as much as said, "She's got you there!"

Nodjme came down to Emily's size and backed away. "Make. Your. Point."

"Happily. So! Instead of leaving us with artifacts such as the pyramids all around the world that we still haven't figured out how the stones were cut, nor how they were put in place, instead of leaving us with numerous self-aggrandizing stone images of yourselves, instead of leaving us with a sphinx, which even now is melting in the climate change with which "my species" is destroying the planet, give us something meaningful.

"This time, you're not to play war, a horrible role-model and shameful legacy to leave. This time you may not be all about your own, quite frankly, embarrassing, egos.

"This time you must work with us. You must teach us the peace and the cooperation you share among yourselves. Give us tools for a true, emotional evolution. Teach us how to love with patience and tolerance. Help us grow up. We need parenting.

"You see, dear goddess, there *is no accident* in my becoming entangled in your agriglyph. I supplicate on behalf of my people. Hear my prayer."

Amenhotep and other gods appeared around Nodjme, forming a half circle of incomprehensible light around them, the plasmoid becoming viscous and glowing. Emily was surprised to realize that she recognized some of these gods. Kings and queens and gods and goddesses, all appearing together, without apparent hierarchy—Tutankhamun, Akhenaten, jackal-headed Anubis, Ramses, Hatshepsut, Isis, Amun, Hathor, Horus, Osiris, ibis-headed Thoth, Nefertiti—each being in a unique, individual light, yet all the light converging into one magnificent, indescribable, transcendent light.

Emily looked at a each of them in turn, "I pray to you, help us help ourselves. This time, it's not a vacation for you, this time, it's a work project. I am supplicating for my people, help us. Teach us how to unlock our sleeping DNA, and how to open the dark, misunderstood, un-accessed recesses of our brains, our minds.

"That's my deal. Agree, or I shan't release my hold on the agriglyph. Kill my little body. Okay, fine. I will continue to plague and nag you. Disembodied, I will be worse."

The gods conferred and Amehotep stepped forward, "Well spoken, little emissary. You have presented impeccable logic. I believe we will comply with your request. Not because you have a hold on Nodjme's agriglyph, but because you bravely risked your life to make an appeal for your people.

"For it is written: 'If there is but one who fearlessly pleads for her people, the gods are duty bound to fulfill that mortal request.'"

A familiar, a terrestrial, sound came to Emily, even as Amenhotep spoke the agreement, which she knew would be upheld. She slowly released her will from the agriglyph, returning to Nodjme that which was hers. In the same moment, she saw Daniel through the sewing room door, it being translucent to her current vision. She saw the keen anxiety in his eyes as he pounded on the door.

As she slowly came to, half in this world, half in another, she discovered that she'd crumpled to the floor. She tasted blood, and blood trickled from her mouth.

Daniel pounded on the door. "Emily?" He called anxiously. "Emily! Are you all right? It sounded like you dropped the sewing machine. Why is the door locked?"

"I'm all right." Emily grabbed a handful of tissues and wiped the blood from her mouth while throwing some yard goods down on the floor to cover the blood. Then she hurried to unlock the door.

Daniel looked at her with uncommon intensity. "What's wrong?"

"Well … I think I … that is … I fainted."

"My god! Why would you do that?"

"Too much excitement around here I guess. I don't know. But don't worry darling. I'm all right, really."

Daniel doted on her so that evening, Emily felt like the Goddess Queen herself. After a light supper—neither of them had much of an appetite, what with the heat and strange disruption to their usual routine—they decided to go out and sit in "their" agriglyph, now that the crowds had dispersed, and the fabulous evening descended.

As they settled in the center of the icon, the sun setting on the western horizon, the evening breeze flared up, and Emily shivered. Daniel hugged her close. She felt safe and warm and at peace. He was a very good man, and hers was indeed an excellent life.

For the first time in her life, she felt nothing but calm contentment.

*   *

Even as the little mortal bodies of Emily and Daniel found peace and companionship and a reason for living on the side of a hill while the sun went down, in another dimension, the agriglyphs united in a great crescendoing apogee. The plasmoids and energies and entities assisting the transmutation of the Goddess Queen Nodjme finally came together with a power beyond human imagination. Colors unlike any that could be seen by human eye, perfumes exceeding the realm of human perceptions, music beyond the range of human hearing cataclysmically rose from earth to stars, and a Goddess was born, again, of flesh and blood.

Nodjme's minions, waiting at the apex of her Nagriglyphs, high above the simple tryst of Emily and Daniel, and rejoicing in the return of their mistress to the three dimensions, wrap her pristine infant body in gossamer translucence, then whisk her in the silent night to her earthly home, to celebrate the pleasure of another turn in the physical realm.

*   *

Which great pleasure is perhaps not so very unlike the pleasure Daniel will experience when he takes his bride to the south of France for a few days to celebrate the new life she carries in the not-to-distant future, in a world suddenly resounding with peace and goodwill. Emily will name the baby Nodjme after some ancient Egyptian Queen. Daniel will wonder why, yet never ask.

But those events are in the future. And mortals may only live one day at a time.

The End

About the Author ....

I live in a forest in the Pacific Northwest with a few domestic and numerous wild creatures, where I create an ever-growing inventory of books and stories.

When you support my work you help support ten acres of natural forest, and all its resident fauna. *All the creatures and I thank you!*

Questions, comments, observations, reviews? I'd love to hear from you!:

Blythe@BlytheAyne.com

www.BlytheAyne.com

First printing: 2018
ISBN: 9781723916861 (2nd Print Edition)

Published by Two Dead Queers
https://twodeadqueers.com

TWO DEAD QUEERS PRESEN[TS]

GUILLOZINE

K.M. CLAUDE & R.E. HELLINGER

TABLE OF CONTENTS

†††

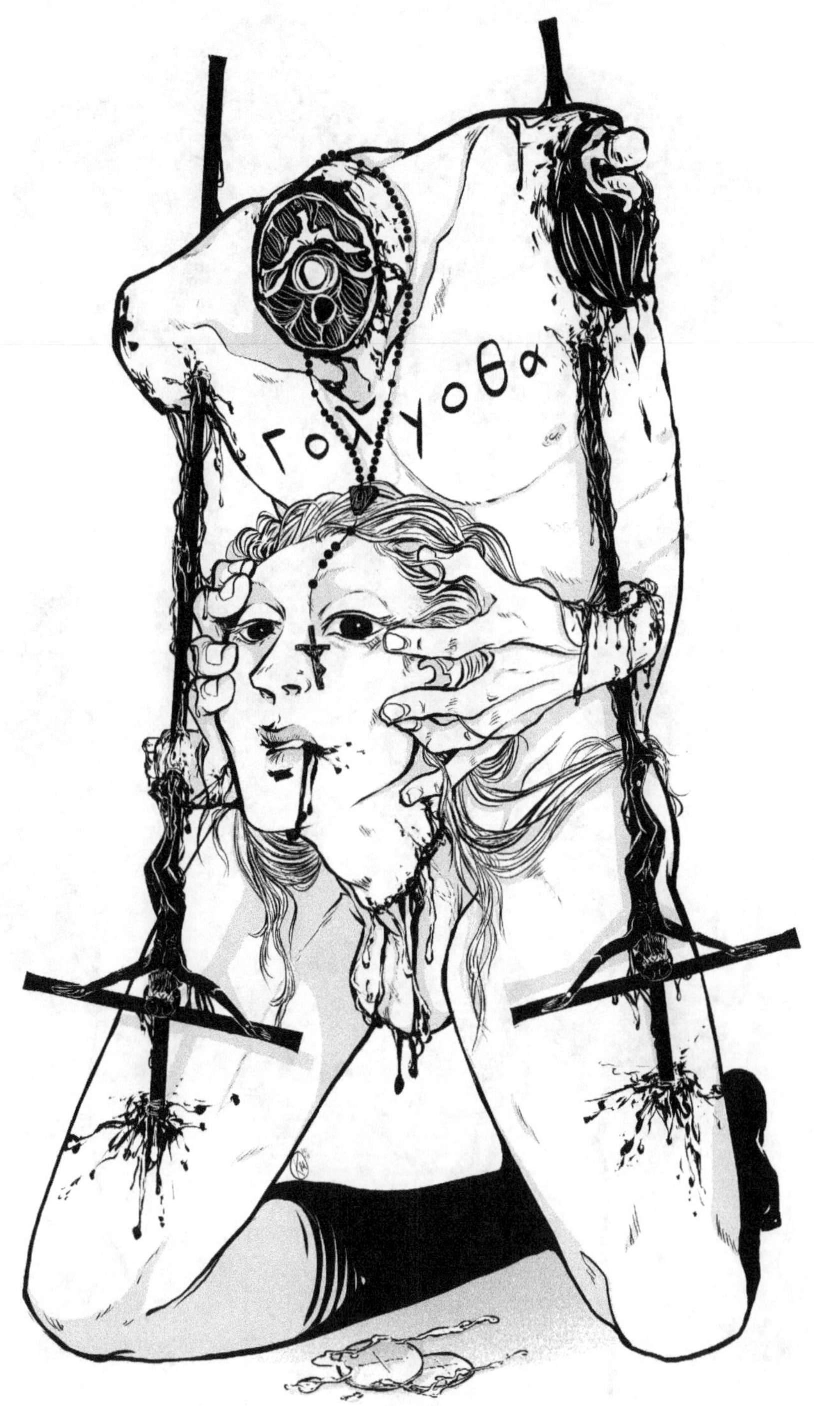
Γολγοθα

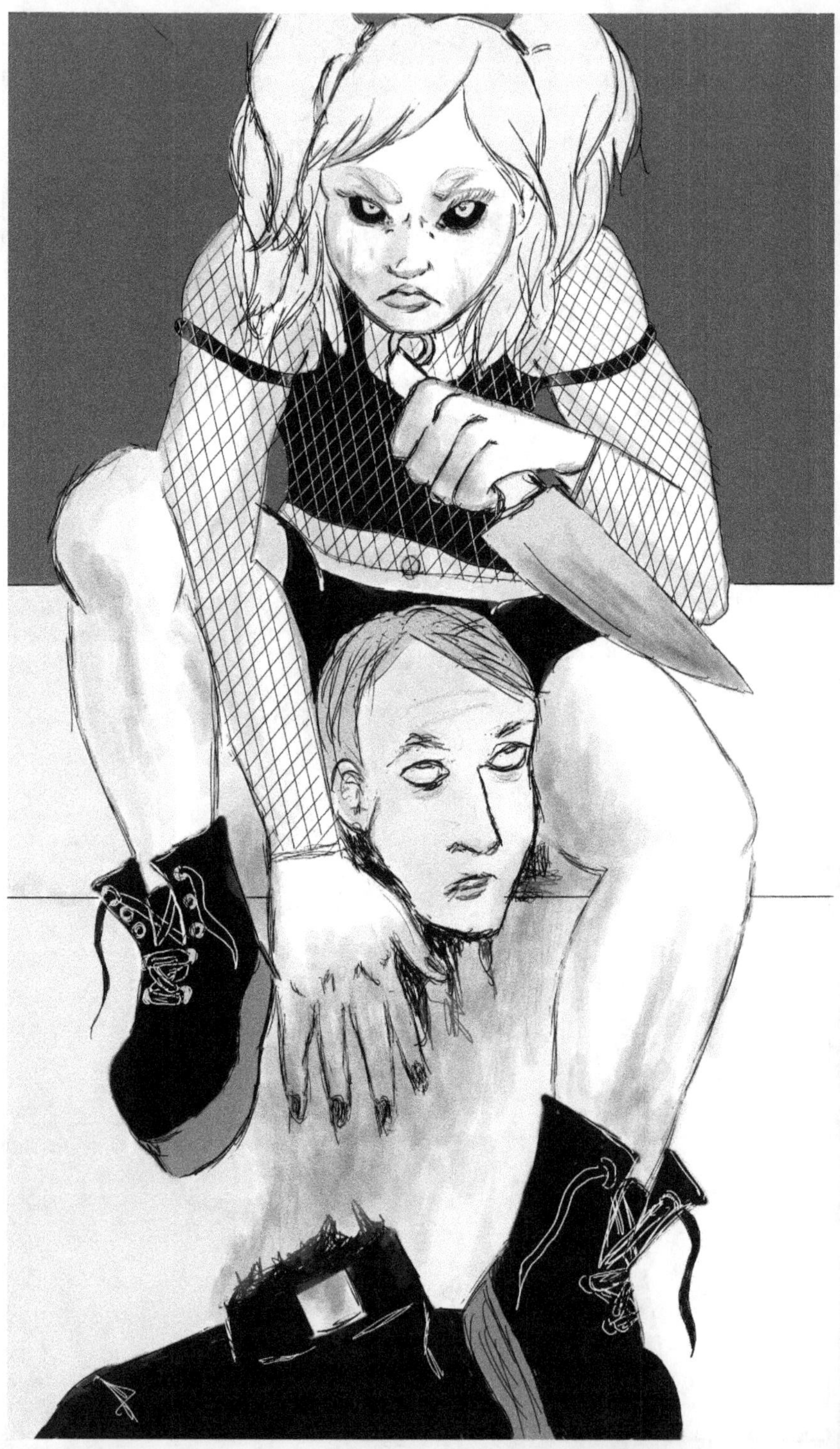

I've been thinking a lot about Judith and Holofernes lately.

Father Constance told me there are many versions, like a fairytale retold and retold. There are many Judiths: swarthy and strong, embittered and determined; but all Holofernes have the face of a monster.

Caravaggio's, hanging in the Galleria Nazionale d'Art Antica in Rome— that's the one I think of. It's the only one I've seen in flesh, but his Judith's arms are my own. They are soft and young, but like me her bones are made of fire.

I stood a long time in front of that painting. I lifted my arm and held it so my forearm was parallel with hers. I made a fist.

I learned a lot that trip, but mostly that my bones could work wonders.

"Do you know what mighty Holofernes did?" Father Constance stood too close to my back when he found me, his voice in my hair, his cassock rough on my bare arms.

I shook my head, eyes tracing the path Judith's blade was carving through Holofernes' neck again. I said,

something terrible. he deserves this.

Constance's eyes and hands fell on my shoulders. A reminder of my holy cage. His thumbs pressed past my hair to rub the raised edges of the Vatican's brand on the back of my neck.

"Let's get you ice cream."

A deep part of me didn't want ice cream. These Vatican men want me obedient and fat and dumb, but I am not two of those things.

I let that coal-becoming-a-diamond part of me press past the promise of sugar and its voice was sharp against my tongue.

does Your God always side with the victor?

Constance's hands tightened on my shoulders. Another reminder. A warning. "With the Righteous."

I let him steer me away from my Judith and toward the man selling gelato in the cafe outside. I asked for cherry topping and made a mess of it so I could lick it from my fingers and the corners of my mouth.

I would never be Righteous, but I could work wonders.

I wanted a knife.

I'D Rather be left alonE IN my hEAD
than be left to Rot
IN tHiS boDy

oh fuck me!

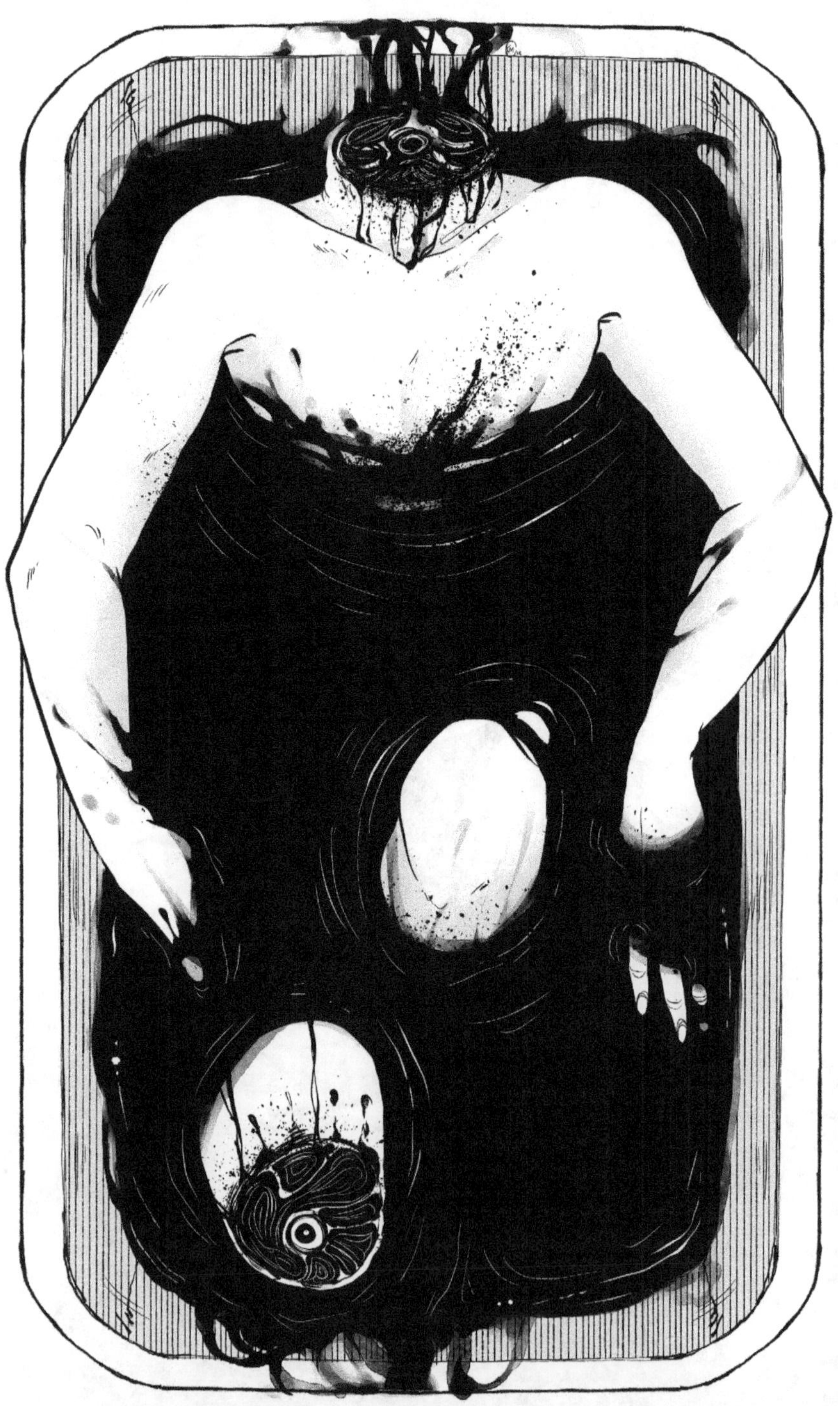

All of young Lord Heath's friends wanted to know how his brother had gotten locked in the family crypt.

"He's always been a deviant," was his answer, and surprisingly everyone agreed. Of course they knew *him*. He, Heath, had been the one who had stayed nearest home—dogging his father's steps, learning the family business, and sometimes tending the blackberry thickets when it wasn't so hot. Hawthorne had always been away, gallivanting back and across the earth, doing God knew *what*. Their father had encouraged it. Perhaps because he'd never gotten along with his own brother he'd felt separation was a healthier rite of passage for growing boys. But it was rumored Hawthorne had been a hedonist, so why not a deviant? The more Heath told the story, the more he believed it himself.

But maybe he wanted to.

"But his own family," Thomas laughed, turning with him into the East wing of the estate. "Somehow that's worse!"

Heath didn't laugh.

Lowering his voice as they drew nearer to a set of tall oak doors, Allan looked at him. "How long was he in there?"

Twisting a key into the lock, Heath pursed his lips as if recalling the stench of the tomb. Instead, the memory of Hawthorne's face—sick with fear as Heath closed one of the innermost cellar doors between them and locked it—swam before him. "Three days."

Pushing the doors open, Heath let them inside. The room was awash in morning sunlight that seemed to touch the wooden shelves and sheer drapes with gold. Gilded titles of books that lined the shelves winked out at them and one of the windows had been opened just slightly so that a breeze lightened the air. Turned so that the breeze was on the side of his face, Hawthorne sat strapped to a wooden wheelchair, looking like a doll that had been discarded.

Heath's friends stopped where they stood and it only occurred to Heath then that his friends had never met Hawthorne before then.

"You're twins!" Thomas blurted.

It wasn't true. Hawthorne was exactly one year older. They shared the same birthday, and thus—as children—had thought to share everything. Their games, their secrets… Suggesting they were twins both drew insidious lines between their true natures and benevolently suggested that Heath was just as entitled to the estate as Hawthorne had been.

They did look remarkably similar. Though, even if Heath cut his brother's hair there would be a division in that Heath could only be described as handsome while his brother—especially now that something had broken inside of him—could only be described as beautiful.

"Come closer, he can't bite."

Allan crossed himself before crossing the threshold, circling the room slowly before he stopped at the other edge of a table that stood near to them. He shook his head slowly. "You should have left him in there, Heath; something doesn't feel right."

Undeterred, Thomas stepped right up to Hawthorne, nearly spitting on him. "Fucking necrophile." Crouching down, he peered up into Hawthorne's slack face, his staring periwinkle eyes. "Why *did* you save him? What good is he?"

Heath laughed thinly from where he stood behind Hawthorne's chair, twisting a strand of Hawthorne's hair between his fingers. "Christ, Thomas, we just lost our father. He's my brother. Does everything need to have a purpose for it to have a place in this world?"

"You forget what he might have been doing to your father in that crypt."

Something flashed in Heath's eyes. "I don't. He's the only living family I have now. Besides," he frowned slightly, using both hands to tilt Hawthorne's head up and back slightly, "He has a *sort of* purpose."

He pulled a black hood from the back of the chair and draped it over Hawthorne's head. Then, without warning, he fisted the fabric tightly in both hands, pulling it back and around the back of Hawthorne's head—so tightly they could see his mouth stretching open against the fabric, straining for air, and the outline of the eye sockets of his skull. He made no sound, but stirred weakly which made it all the more worse to watch.

Eyes full of a strange light, Heath looked down at where Thomas was still crouched before his brother. "Who do you want to talk to?"

Thomas shook his head, at a loss. "What?"

"Anyone that's gone before."

"Heath…"

"Choose."

"My…great aunt?" Thomas looked from the twisting skull like visage before him, screaming silently behind its veil.

"Say her name so she can hear you."

"Marie… Marie Anne Withrows."

At once Hawthorne grew still. Heath slowly released the fabric so that the screaming face disappeared, but left the hood on his brother's head.

It felt as though someone was walking around them, behind them in the room, pacing like a cautious observer.

Thomas turned his face anxiously up to the hooded face and from behind the fabric a soft voice crept forth—muted and wavering like a candle's flame—but undeniably that of an Irish woman.

"Tommy, is that you?"

†††

They supped in the parlor, as the dining room was far too big for the three of them. Thomas had agreed to stay on the condition that Hawthorne remain behind the locked doors of the study. He couldn't stomach seeing the slack face from which his great aunt had spoken. And he *did* believe. As he explained, helping himself to some cold chicken and blackberries without much relish, no one outside of his family knew they had Irish blood in them. Not even their priest.

"It's a grave power you have at your fingertips," Allan said slowly. He'd lit a cigarette and had been musing. Leaned back in his chair away from the table with his ankle crossed over his knee, he almost looked like a dandy. Thomas had said as much and got a smoke ring to the face for it. Fixing his eyes on Heath, Allan arched an eyebrow. "You could make a lot of coin off of this."

Heath laughed. "And have to deal with that Spiritist lot? No thanks."

Thomas still looked gray from his encounter. He seemed tired and shook his head more at his plate than at anything else. "I wouldn't sell that. I don't think men would know whether to drink or ask for their money back after that sort of parlor trick."

Allan ashed his cigarette into his teacup, sneering. "It's a service."

"I don't suppose you're going to ask for a refund?"

Thomas fixed his gaze on Heath for a long moment, then he sighed. "If I could have the entire memory erased by asking, I might." Standing, he gathered his coat and hat and tapped at the brim of it lightly, weighing his words. "I've got to get back to town; I've got a dinner appointment with

Carmichael and a lot of gin."

He shared a ghost of a smile with all of them and, winking, went to the door where he paused anew. "It's not that I regret it— But I'm glad I didn't call anyone closer to me."

With a significant look at Heath and a casual bow of his head, he left and his footsteps echoed down the hall.

Allan laughed and helped himself to Thomas' tea. "He's just mad we found out he's a filthy Irish. This gift is wasted on wanting to speak to dead relatives, anyway."

Heath's eyes were on the door. His mind was with his brother's haunted temple of a body. "What do you mean?"

Putting out his cigarette, Allan moved his chair closer and dropped his voice. "Spiritists focus on resolution. On easing the mind. It's so stuffy and tired. Not one of them sees all it could be: that we could play and laugh anew with the dead.

"How many men would pay to see their wives again, touch their mistresses again, *bed Cleopatra* for Christ's sake?"

Heath turned his attention to him. "Are you asking me to run a brothel out of my own estate where men can pay to bed my *brother*?"

Allan was unfazed. "You said yourself he was headless. Just a body with an incredible gift. Besides, what better justice for his deviance than to be a tool for the living to commune with the dead? It's far holier than what he was doing.

"He wanted the dead for their rotting, carnal bodies. We want his body for spiritual renewal with our dearly departed."

Heath stared.

Leaning his chin into his palm, Allan smiled, eyes heavy from the opium in his cigarette. "I'll pay handsomely."

†††

The sun had long since set behind the advent of a storm and now lightning crackled beyond the window's glass. For a moment Heath found himself holding his breath. There was nothing to fear *here*, of course. Here, together, they were safe.

The bathroom was lit generously with candles and Heath had undressed and placed his brother in the clawfoot tub by the windows. He sat behind him on the edge of a chair, sleeves rolled to his elbows, hands lathered in soap and buried in Hawthorne's hair.

"Do you remember," Heath asked, carding his fingers through his brother's wet hair slowly, leaning close to the shell of his ear, "When we found that thing in the cellars as children?"

"We'd gone down," he recounted slowly, almost lazily as he began to rinse the soap from Hawthorne's hair. "Much further than we should have. Past the second set of doors, and the third…

"We had father's key, so we didn't care how many doors there were so long as they would open. We lost count and the passages kept narrowing and going down and down. Father had told us how old this place was, but not how deeply they'd dug the foundations. I don't even know if he knew.

"And then we found *it* behind the old stained press and it was hungry. You were scared; it wanted you the most and you knew it. It seemed blind yet it followed us, pulling itself along, writhing on its belly, not so much screaming as sighing."

He stopped, his fingers trailing limply in the water behind his brother's back. Drawing a breath, he laughed and it seemed to shake the chill off of him as he began to scoop palms of water up over Hawthorne's shoulders, watching it run down his back in rivulets. "Do you remember? They would have organized a search party if father hadn't already known where we'd gone. It felt like hours, running for our lives, tripping, picking one another back up. We dropped the lantern at one point and just kept going.

"I don't know how we made it back but father was waiting at the top of the cellar stairs with a shovel. Like he'd been waiting for this to happen.

"You didn't watch, but he savaged it. I saw the whole thing— Most of it.

"He beheaded it and hit it over and over and over with that shovel until you could no longer tell what parts had been arms and what bits had been even remotely human. Whatever it was, he scooped it up the remaining slop and took it away.

"Did you ever ask him what he did with it? I did. Once. And do you know what he said to me? That he'd burnt it and scattered the ashes far, far away."

Leaning ever closer, lips brushing the back of Hawthorne's ear, he smiled. "But we both know he didn't. I think he dumped its mangled leavings in that old press. Did you look while you were down there day and night? I hope you did. I hope it watched you. I knew it was down there somewhere... The air at the top of the cellar steps was never empty after we found it.

"You should have chosen me!" He snarled, pulling back on Hawthorne's hair as if reining in a horse. Hawthorne's mindless eyes gazed heavenward at the ceiling.

Panting Heath looked down at him, shaking his head, recalling the absolute fear that had lined Hawthorne's face when there should have been understanding and desire. How drunk they'd been after their father's funeral, holding hands as they went down to the cellar to face what they hadn't been able to as children, laughing… How soft and willing Hawthorne had looked when Heath turned to him by the lantern light in that final room. He'd even let Heath press him back against the wall, his pale eyes had locked onto Heath's lips, smiling.

But when Heath had suggested they could have whatever they wanted—that father was gone, and they could run the family estate together… When he'd brushed Hawthorne's cheek with his thumb and kissed him in that room full of rot and shadows, Hawthorne closed himself off to Heath.

Frightened, shaking his head, he'd gently pushed Heath away and that was when the estate passed from Hawthorne to Heath and their future together ended forever.

Hawthorne's beauty hurt. To touch, but not to ever actually *have* him, Heath's one truest friend and confidant—was agony.

The bathroom was silent and still save for the flicker of the candles under the mirror. In its reflection, Hawthorne didn't even bat an eye. He stared resolutely past some point on the wall.

Still gazing at their reflection, Heath laid his chin on Hawthorne's shoulder, leaning his head against his throat. He slid fingertips down the front of Hawthorne's chest, watching as not even his muscles reacted to the featherlight contact. For once in his life, he had the money, the name, and the wits in hand while Hawthorne didn't. Sighing, he allowed a smile to flicker across his face and slipped his fingers between Hawthorne's waiting legs, enjoying his warmth, his *placidity*.

"We're going to play a little game tomorrow with a friend," he said, stroking his brother's cock, amused that his deviant brother would never be aroused again—by anything, "Something new, and if you disappoint me in any way, I'll give you over to it. It'll let it finish what I started after father died. I'll let it undo the rest of you: body and soul, like it's been wanting to all these years."

His eyes narrowed as he studied where their similarities met and their differences separated them. Physically, aside from their style and manner, they were nearly twins. Other than that, well… The difference was all in their heads.

†††

The morning brought bad news from the thickets. Some of Heath's men had come across something viscous and dark near the roots of a bush, smeared in the dirt. Taking their knives, they'd cut one sliver and then another out of the plant only to find the same dark mess inside. They came into the house immediately to report it to Heath as he took his coffee in the library and presented him with the evidence.

Heath left to look at the material himself.

Like sap, it was thick but not sticky, though it stained and stunk a good deal. None of the men had ever seen anything like it and, wrapping a section of a branch in packaging paper and tying it with twine, Heath sent a man off to London with it and a letter for a friend of the family's who had served as their father's botanist. Certainly, if it were some sort of virus or fungus, he would know.

By the time Heath had set a solution for the misfortune in motion and washed the slime and its horrid dark stain from his hands, he came downstairs to find Allan waiting for him in the parlor.

They passed the afternoon hunting and riding. After supper, Heath sent the house staff to bed, and lighting a candle, led Allan to Hawthorne's room. He'd laid him out in a clean nightshirt and brushed his hair out against the pillow. In the still, silent way his body waited, Heath had the impression of a giant, awful doll that knew what was coming.

Heath swallowed back a lump that had risen in his throat and handed Allan the black hood he'd used to call up Thomas' great-aunt.

"I've given him opium to make him more docile, just in case."

"Perfect," Allan said. His eyes were carving a line down Hawthorne's body.

"You know how to use it?" Heath touched the hood.

Allan frowned down at it as if it, alone, was the distasteful part of the whole process. "Can't I just use my hands?"

There was bile in Heath's throat now. Images of Allan's

fingers squeezing what life remained in Hawthorne out of his body flooded into his mind unchecked. Allan's face was cruel in these images: Hawthorne's eyes frightened, the bed rocking, Hawthorne's body lifting and crashing effortlessly against the mattress again and again.

"You could, but it will help not to see his face. The spirit speaking through his face will be...strange. Who are you calling forth, anyway?"

"A whore I fucked last summer," Allan said, stretching out a finger to stroke Hawthorne's exposed wrist slowly, his mind elsewhere, lost in summer. "Died of consumption."

So I truly am running a brothel, then, Heath thought. "That's too bad."

He wanted away from the candlelight that highlighted the pearlescence of Hawthorne's skin. Wanted a door between himself and Allan's lust.

"Remember to state the woman's name clearly," he advised, stopping at the door and turning. "Oh, and Allan: please don't need anything more from me before morning."

Allan laughed loudly, but even as Heath closed the door behind him, he couldn't escape the sight of Allan climbing on top of his brother, pulling the hood over his head.

Swallowing bile, Heath's hands shook as he pulled the door shut. His fingers trembled too badly to fit the skeleton key in the lock and turn it so he retreated to the study where he poured himself a large glass of brandy.

It wouldn't have been the first time he'd seen Hawthorne with a man. He could still recall the summer afternoon he'd stumbled across his brother with a man from their hunting party. The party got separated, and when Heath's half of the party determined their horses had had enough for the day, Heath went to look for them on his own.

He found them in a glen just beyond the thickets, well hidden by trees and brush. In this sun dappled clearing, spread like an eager whore, Hawthorne laughed as the man called him his little fox and squeezed his hips with hands larger and rougher than Heath's. Instead of making his presence known, Heath stayed hidden, watching as the man fucked Hawthorne roughly, the two of them hissing and growling like animals. Hawthorne pushed the man out of him before he came, saying he didn't want any of his seed on his riding clothes and the man came on a patch of wildflowers beside them, grumbling. Then Hawthorne came on the man's thigh and they fell into a tangle of limbs as they wrestled and kissed.

Half hard, Heath had crept away. Hawthorne's raucous laughter rose behind him until he was halfway home, shaming him.

Tonight was similar, and though Heath contented himself with the fact that Allan could only help himself to the mere shell of Hawthorne it was a fragile comfort.

Heath drank from his glass deeply, eyes locked on the lithe, dancing body of a candle's flame at the opposite side of the study. He imagined Hawthorne: naked, standing at the end of his bed, hands moving over his body, presenting himself to Heath. In his mind, Hawthorne hummed a half-remembered fugue, body twisting and arching dreamlike.

"Come here," Heath whispered to the empty room. The candle stayed put but his imaginary Hawthorne smiled and crawled up over him, straddling his hips, letting Heath touch and explore him, going so far as to suck the finger Heath slid between his lips.

Heath grunted as he imagined the softness of Hawthorne's skin and the gentle weight of his eyes on him, his body open to him without fear or hesitation. Closing his eyes, Heath took his cock in hand and quickly worked himself to a feverish pace. His mind took him to the glen, then to Allan straddling Hawthorne only minutes ago. He imagined himself pushing Hawthorne down the cellar stairs again and again, imagined

taking him in that deepest cellar by lantern light even as
Hawthorne tried to push him off. It was his right. Their right.
Their father wasn't there to tell them it was wrong; their
friends weren't there to call them abominable. Who else had
been there for them? Who else could love wild, twisted boys
raised from thickets like them, besides one another?

His imaginary Hawthorne smiled, fingers touching his
cheek and Heath turned his face to kiss those invisible fingers,
coming into his own hand in the study alone.

Catching his breath, he watched the candle dance and
seemingly wink. He thought he heard Hawthorne's breathy
laugh in his ear, but he was tired and the brandy was pulling
him down, down, and so he slept.

†††

His dreams were stormy and turbulent. At one moment,
he'd been Allan instead of himself, bedding Hawthorne, but
Hawthorne was weeping beneath the black hood and so he
stopped rocking his hips and leaned down over him, lifting
the fabric...

Then he was in the middle of the blackberry orchards
and the brambles had gone all but wild, making it difficult
to traverse. Hawthorne was running somewhere ahead of
him, only in his nightshirt, blood or berry-stained from the
waist down. Whatever had infected his thickets had made the
ground thick and sinking, and it crept up Heath's riding boots
as he ran. As a storm brewed overhead, skies darkening, he
stopped, realizing he'd lost Hawthorne entirely. He called for
him, but received no reply—only the growing sensation that
he was being watched from all sides.

Turning, he took a blackberry between his fingers and slit
it open with the tip of his hunting knife.

A rolling black eye stared back at him. The black-red

muck of the fields was up to his calves.

Gasping, he found himself back over Hawthorne in the bed and Hawthorne was screaming, fingers gripping at his chest, tears coursing down his cheeks. Hawthorne's eyes rolled back and a black eye stared up at Heath from the darkness at the back of Hawthorne's throat. "It's blood! It's all built on blood!"

Heath woke up, gasping. He'd thrown his half empty glass of brandy to the floor at some point and the deep red liquid had left a gash on the Persian rug.

It must have been about two in the morning, and the threads of his dreams still clung to him. Shaking himself, he forced himself to listen to the black silence wrapped around the manor. He thought he'd heard a scream and couldn't be sure it hadn't been his own.

Somewhere on the other side of the study, he got the distinct feeling like something was pacing, watching, invisible. There was an almost palpable sadness; an urgency—

The candle at the far side of the study flickered then went out.

"Hawthorne?"

The silence of the night was torn in two by a scream and then another—high and wet, like a pig's squeal.

Heath was on his feet in an instant and followed after the sound as it carried him back to Hawthorne's room. The door was closed and something red and sharp rose up inside of him. If Allan had done anything to his brother—

As his hand closed around the doorknob, he was almost pulled into the room as Allan came crashing out, one hand gripping the front of his throat. He grabbed at Heath's shoulder, eyes wild. He was still wearing his black riding breeches, but the rest of him that was bare was slathered in blood.

"It wasn't her— I used the hood, I covered his head, I said

her name, I did it right, but it wasn't her." He was babbling. "He— *It* bit me. It!" He swung an accusing finger into the candlelit room and Heath used the moment to gently move Allan's hand away from his throat and took a stunned step back.

A large bite had been taken out of Allan's throat and tatters of skin still hung in ribbons where teeth had torn savagely at the flesh. There was so much blood, an artery must have been severed. He was dimly aware that Allan was turning back towards him, that his clammy hand was closing over one of his, that he was trying to say something else, but Heath was too busy watching Allan's Adam's apple bob without the privacy of skin covering it. Blood bubbling from his neck, Allan swooned and fell to the floor where he lay still. A pool of blood spread slowly from him. Stepping over it, Heath took a deep breath and pushed into the room.

Hawthorne's body was sitting up on the bed, his hooded head turned towards the door as if expecting Heath. His nightshirt was stained with Allan's blood and by the candlelight, Heath could see something wet on the front of the hood, and felt eyes on him.

Whatever had bitten Allan was still here, behind the hood, inside of his brother's body and as he neared the bed he thought he could see where Allan had gone wrong.

He *had* used the hood, but he had also tied a length of velvet cord around and around the base of the hood to strangle Hawthorne. Hawthorne, then, must be dead.

The heaviness of the thought settled so hard in the pit of his stomach that when the thing gibbered at him—chattering the teeth that it had pushed through the fabric like cursed pearls to bite Allan—he swung the back of his hand against its face and brought his foot down on its ribs as it fell off the bed in a heap.

"You want my brother? Rot in his body!"

Grabbing the top of the hood and the luscious

hair gathered under it, Heath dragged the thing inside Hawthorne's body out of the room and through the spreading pool of Allan's blood, bringing the stain with them down the hallway.

The thing inside Hawthorne raged—thrashing and twisting in his grip—but though it pushed its tongue against the thick fabric of the hood and clacked its horrible teeth at Heath, it didn't so much scream as sigh hotly.

Kicking open the door to the cellar, Heath lifted it and threw it bodily down the stairs where it twisted and writhed its way to the bottom. It almost hurt to see Hawthorne like that: his limbs twisted and twitching on stonework.

Meeting it at the bottom, he rolled it over with his foot, onto its back. Taking a shovel from the wall, he brought the spade end down where the coarse fabric of the hood ended and Hawthorne's silken skin began. The body lay silent and still.

Wiping sweat from his brow, Heath brought Hawthorne's wheelchair down to the basement, tied the body to it and sat the head in its lap, then walked it back to the furthest reaches of the basement. Who knew this basement better than them, of course? He went through one door with his skeleton key, then another, then another, stopping only when the foundations around them were old and wet with the earthen stain eating his blackberries.

In a room with the old stained press and bottles that were so time-gnawed the liquid inside of them looked like it had congealed into thick, black rot, he left his brother and the monster that had wanted Hawthorne more than he had.

He locked every door behind him.

†††

Of course, Allan's death was easy to explain. Hawthorne's

health had come back and he'd attacked their houseguest, leaving him for dead before he ran madly out into the moors.

Heath sent his house staff out to look for him, but no traces were ever found.

The fungus faded from the fields like a bad dream and time moved on and Heath filled his life with new things: a wife, new hunting dogs, a set of twin boys. He named one after his brother, of course.

But like all young boys, they found their way into trouble often enough—in the thickets, in the house… Looking back, Heath should have known simply beheading it and locking it down in the deepest cellar wouldn't be enough. When his sons came up from the cellars breathless and pale, crying about something that sighed and didn't so much crawl as pull itself along—sightless, dragging a dark rope—knotted bag along beside it, Heath wondered how the hell their father had had the stomach to kill his own brother twice.

He went and got his shovel.

This time, he'd burn and scatter him—far away. Separation was good for growing boys, of course. He'd do what their father had never had the heart to do: let go of his brother completely.

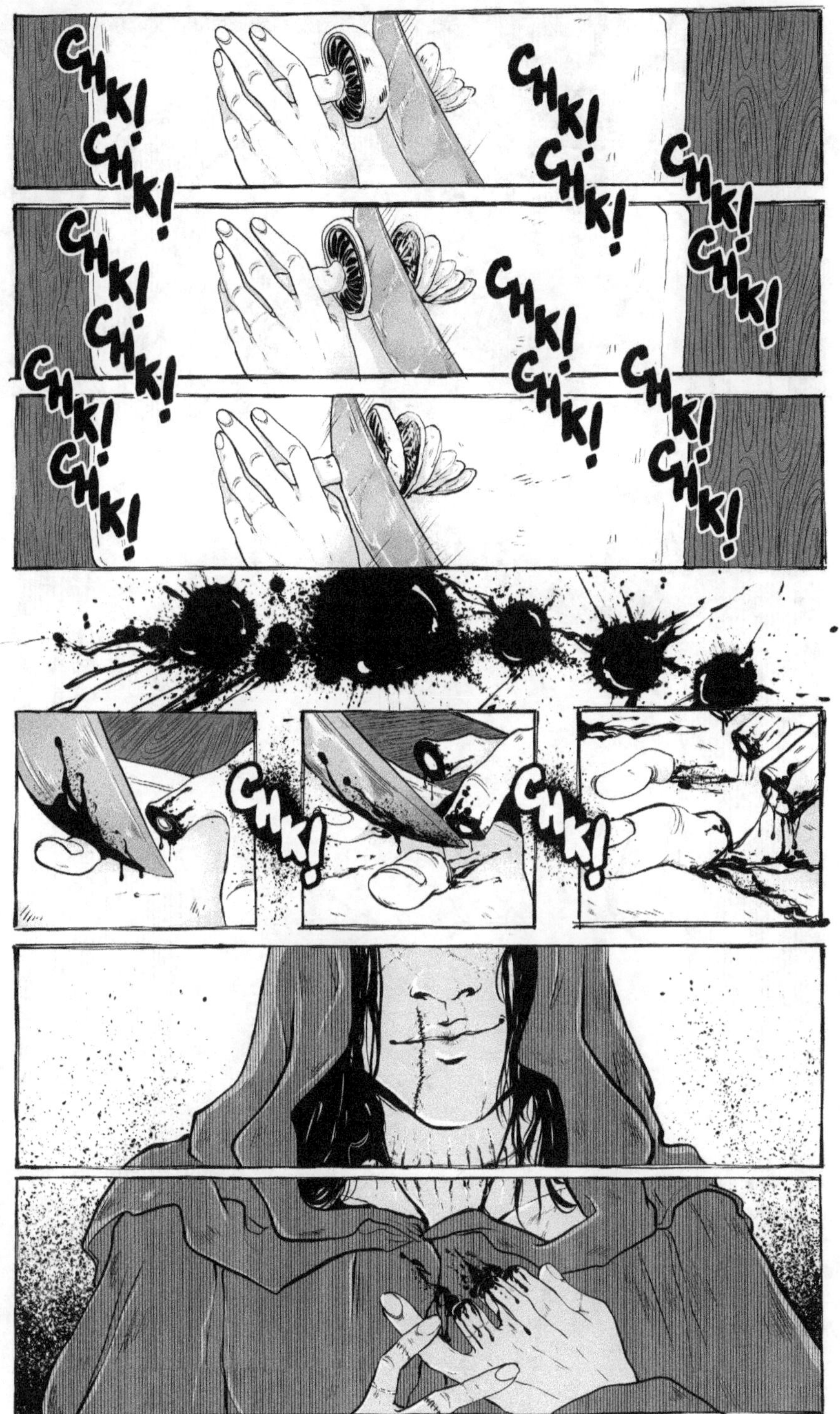

CHK!
CHK!
CHK!
CHK!
CHK!
CHK!
CHK!
CHK!
CHK!
CHK!
CHK!
CHK!
CHK!

BORN HEADLESS
AND THE REST'S
A DRAG!

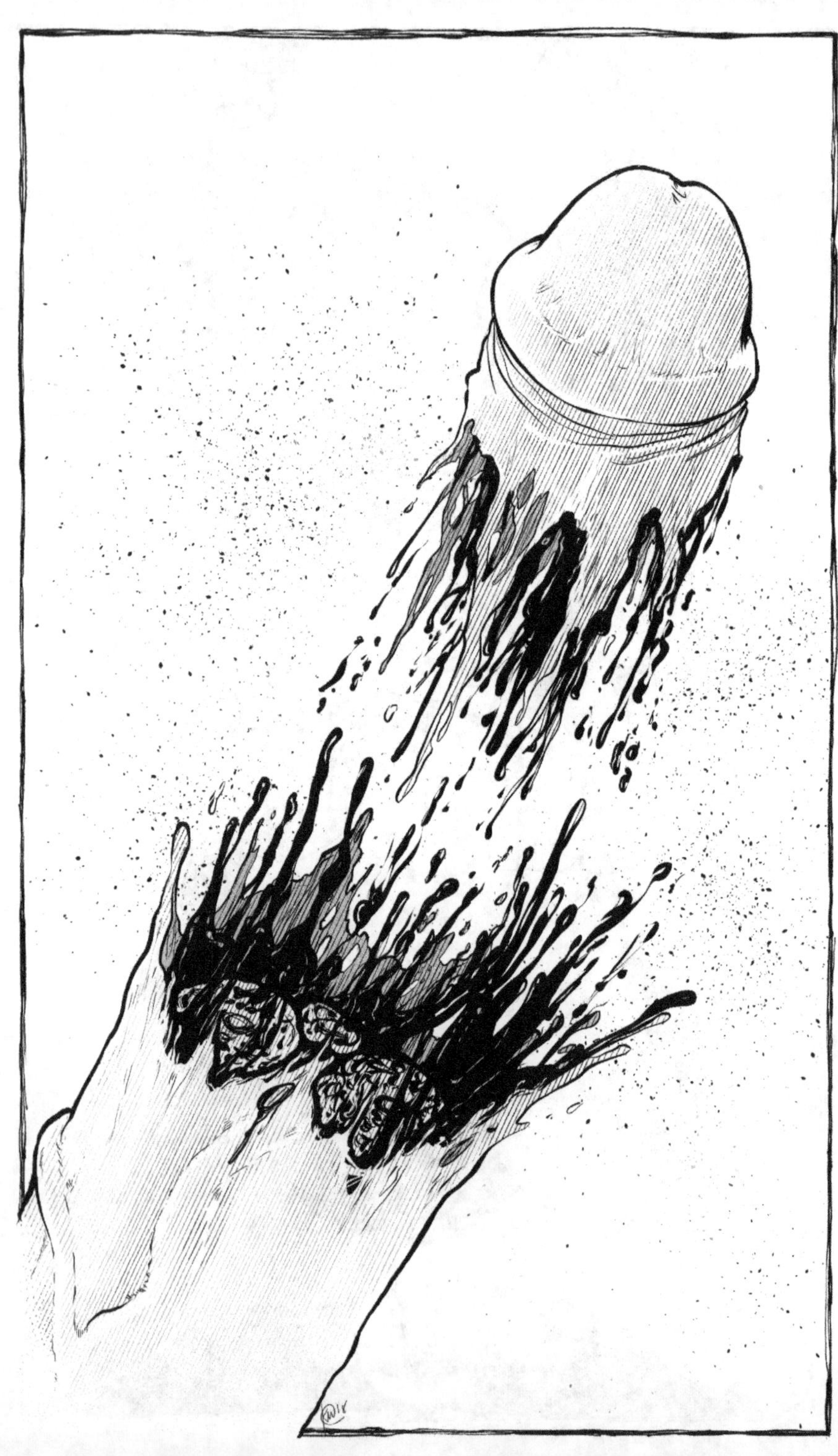

ABOUT THE AUTHORS

Known for the religious horror graphic novel *Ninety-Nine Righteous Men* and the mind behind nonSENSE Press' *NANSENSU* anthologies,

K. M. CLAUDE

is a queer indie horror and erotica cartoonist creating comics, zines, and other works of art that glorify the grotesque, delight in the deviant, and sexualize the sordid.

Find him on
kmclaude.com

Hailing from the kudzu-smothered south,

R.E. HELLINGER

has long been a fan of all things spooky and ooky. When they're not swindling mortal souls in crossroads deals or texting Claude about their cat Saint, they can be found doing—well—this. You can follow their misadventures on Twitter **@roanofarc.**

This is their first creative publication.

† TWO DEAD QUEERS PRESENT: GUILLOZINE †

www.ingramcontent.com/pod-product-compliance
Lightning Source LLC
Chambersburg PA
CBHW061103050726
47592CB00004B/1807

9 781723 916861